FLASH 50

NEW QUICK FICTION

DON TASSONE

TOERNER PRESS

Paperback ISBN 979-8-218-51227-9

Cover design by Maggie Toerner

For Liz

"There is no greater agony than bearing an untold story inside you."

MAYA ANGELOU

CONTENTS

PREFACE

No doubt flash fiction has come on strong because it's a quick read in these busy times.

But flash fiction stories can also convey deep truths and universal human emotions in just a few short paragraphs. They can offer more than brevity. They can be thought-provoking. They can nourish.

I hope you find the 50 new flash fiction stories in this collection thought-provoking and nourishing.

Don Tassone
November 2024

YESTERDAY

STARRY, STARRY NIGHT

I'D BEEN CONGESTED and coughing all day when my wife suggested I take a Covid test.

"Nobody tests anymore," I said.

"But if you've got it, you'll spread it," she said.

I knew she was right. I had a week full of meetings and events ahead. I didn't want to cancel anything, but I didn't want to infect anyone either.

So I took the test. It was positive.

I cancelled my appointments for the week. Suddenly, I was homebound with an open calendar. I wasn't sure what I was going to do.

Then an idea came to mind. A few days earlier, I'd heard Don McLeans's "Starry, Starry Night" on the radio. It was still playing in my head. It made me think of Van Gogh's famous painting. And that made me think of the paint by numbers I did as a kid. Maybe I should do one now to pass the time, I thought.

So I went online, found a paint by number of "The Starry

Night" and ordered it. It arrived in a long, thin box the following day.

I cleared the dining room table and opened the box. Tucked inside were a 16 by 20-inch rolled-up canvas, instructions, strips of little plastic paint pots, several brushes and a little poster of the finished painting to use as a guide.

I was surprised there were so many numbered sections: 1,205. I hadn't noticed that online. This was a lot more involved and advanced than the paint by numbers I did as a kid. Maybe this wasn't such a good idea, I thought.

I read the instructions. They laid out the process in a simple, orderly fashion: paint in sections, top to bottom, left to right, light colors to dark. They also included "pro tips."

The first tip was to tape down the edges of the canvas on a flat surface. I grabbed a roll of masking tape and did that. Seeing the whole gamut of tiny numbered sections made my task seem even more daunting.

For a moment, I felt an urge to stuff everything back in the box and return it. But then what would I do all week?

I popped open the little paint cup stamped "1." White. I checked out all the "1" sections in the upper left corner of the canvas, selected the smallest-tipped brush and dipped it in. Then I slowly lowered the tip of the brush to a small section near the corner and began to fill it in.

I tried to stay inside the lines. But after only a few strokes, my brush strayed into a different section.

In that moment, I was transported back to my childhood and an experience I had nearly forgotten.

When I was six years old, my mother bought me a paint-by-number kit. It was an autumn scene filled with trees bursting with color.

She set up a card table in my bedroom, laid out the contents of the kit and brought in a small glass of water so I could clean my brush between colors. She told me what to do, then left me to paint on my own.

But as soon as I started painting, I screwed up. I couldn't stay inside the lines, and the colors began to run together.

I pounded my fist on the table and stood up fast, knocking my chair over. Through tears, I glared down at my awful handiwork.

"I can't do this!" I yelled.

I grabbed the cardboard canvas, tore it in half and stuffed it in my trash can.

My mother must have heard all the commotion because she came back into my room. I was sitting on my bed, crying.

She sat down next to me.

"What's wrong?" she said.

"I can't paint!"

"Why do you say that?"

I told her what had happened. I thought she'd be upset. Instead, she said, "You don't have to stay inside the lines, you know. Artists blend colors. They blend everything. That's what makes their paintings so beautiful."

If I'd been older, I might have thought she was just saying that to make me feel better. But I took her words to heart.

"Do you want to try another painting sometime?" she said.

"Maybe," I said, sniffing.

"Well, whenever you'd like, we can go to the store and pick one out."

A few days later, we went to Kmart, and I picked out a new paint-by-number kit: a spring scene with lots of blossoms and flowers.

When we got home, my mother helped me set up again. Then, once again, she left my room.

I sat down and began to paint. This time, though, I didn't get flustered when my brush strayed outside the lines.

A few days later, I finished that painting, which I proudly showed my family. My mother framed it, and together we hung it on my bedroom wall.

Now I scanned the nearly blank canvas on my dining room table, then studied the poster of the finished painting.

I remembered reading a story about Van Gogh painting "The Starry Night" after looking out the window from his room in an asylum and seeing a large morning star. He wasn't allowed to paint in his room, so he began painting the star he'd seen in a studio, without the view for reference. The result was a dream-like image, a combination of elements real and imagined.

I thought about my life. I never imagined I'd be so successful in the corporate world. Many of my colleagues have been smarter than me. But unlike most of them, I've always been able to navigate ambiguity, and that has made all the difference.

"Artists blend everything." All my life, I've heard my mother's voice and felt her loving presence.

I finished all the "1" sections, with white paint bleeding beyond many of the lines, and moved onto "2." Blue, my mother's favorite color.

THE GREETING

REALIZING he was about to die, David was terrified. There had always been time, but no longer. He'd put off Confession, and now, unable to speak, he was about to pay the awful price.

He'd begged God's forgiveness, but he'd also been taught mortal sins must be confessed properly. He was so ashamed, though, that he'd never been able to speak to anyone about his transgressions, not even a priest.

Now everything was dark, and David wanted to scream. Then everything was light, and he felt someone embrace him and say in a voice so warm, "Welcome, David. I love you."

MATTERS OF THE HEART

REASON WAS BORN BRILLIANT. Maybe his parents somehow knew that when they named him.

Watching Reason grow up was a study in logic. In the first grade, when most kids were learning basic math, Reason was doing algebra. In high school, he won the Harvard-MIT Math Tournament. In college, he double majored in physics and computer science. He went on to earn advanced degrees in astrophysics and work for NASA.

Reason's pursuits were usually intellectual. He didn't like sports and had no interest in fashionable clothes. He was plain-looking and shy. He never asked anyone out, and women seemed to have no interest in him.

But people admired Reason. He was modest, earnest and kind. And his brilliance wowed everyone, even in the rarefied atmosphere of NASA.

Still, Reason kept to himself. One day, while he was reading a book over lunch in the cafeteria, much to his surprise, a pretty young woman came over and sat down next to him.

She introduced herself. Her name was Cora. She didn't ask Reason about his work or talk about hers. She wanted to know where he was from. She asked about his family and his interests. She wanted to know about him, not as a rocket scientist, but as a person.

Reason was captivated by Cora. He'd never met anyone like her, and by the end of that lunch, he'd begun to fall in love.

A year later, Reason and Cora were married. On their honeymoon, lying beside Cora, Reason said, "So what was it that led you to sit down next to me in the cafeteria that day?"

"What do you think?" she said with a smile.

"My mind?"

"Yes."

"And what about when you came back the next day?"

"By then, it was your heart."

THE JOY OF LISTENING

SONSOLES' patients called her "The Listener" because of how well she always listened to them.

Growing up, Sonsoles was shy. She lacked self confidence. She felt ignored.

But as a teenager, Sonsoles began to shine. She was smart. After college, she went to medical school and became an ENT surgeon.

Ten years into her career, Sonsoles stunned the world by discovering a cure for deafness.

She was awarded the Nobel Prize for Medicine. In accepting it, she said, "My discovery came not from any special skills, but by knowing the sadness of not being heard and the joy of listening."

REKINDLED

MARY AND BEN were The Lodge Retirement Community's newest residents. Both had recently lost their spouses. Their hearts were broken. Their inner fires had gone out.

Ben was sitting alone in the dining room, having dinner. Mary was about to find a table of her own when she saw him.

"Would you mind some company?" she said.

"Not at all," he said.

"Thank you."

She parked her walker and sat down.

"I'm Mary," she said, extending her hand.

"I'm Ben," he said, taking it.

A waitress came over and took Mary's order. Ben stopped eating to wait for her dinner to be served.

"Please keep eating," Mary said.

"I'm happy to wait," Ben said.

Once they'd both said where they were from and that their spouses had recently died, Mary said, "So what did you do for a living?"

"I was a carpenter," Ben said.

"How wonderful."

"I was a wood carver too."

"Really? What kind of things did you carve?"

As Mary's dinner was served, Ben told her about his carvings, from spoons and snowmen and to fruit and animals.

"Did you ever carve a lamb?" she said.

"No, I don't think so. Why do you ask?"

"Joe was a good man," she said, talking about her late husband. "But he wasn't perfect. He told me he'd committed sins, although he never told me what they were. As he lay dying, he kept asking for a lamb. I wasn't sure what he meant. He told me if he could just hold a lamb, he knew he would be forgiven. But I had nothing to give him, and he died empty-handed."

"I'm sorry," Ben said.

After a moment of silence, Mary said, "Do you think you could carve a small lamb for me?"

"I would," Ben said, "but I'm afraid my woodworking days are over."

"Why?"

"I have arthritis, and my hands shake."

"I see," Mary said, looking sad.

After dinner, Ben went back to his room. He sat in his recliner and thought about Mary's story and her question. *Do you think you could carve a small lamb for me?* He wondered why she wanted it. After all, her husband was now gone.

He hadn't carved anything in years. But he still had his tools and several blocks of basswood. He'd seen his daughter put his tool bag in his bedroom closet when she was moving him in.

He pushed his walker into his bedroom, pulled his tool bag out of his closet and set it on his walker. Then he pushed his walker out to his small dining table and slid his tool bag onto the table.

He sat down, unzipped the bag and pulled out the fabric roll where he kept his carving tools. He untied it and spread it flat on the table. Then he reached back into his bag and pulled out a four-inch block of basswood.

He ran his fingers over the smooth surface of the wood, closed his eyes and thought about all the things he had fashioned from wood over the years: furniture, cabinets, planters, intricate objects for his wife Ruth, toys for their children and grandchildren, a nativity scene Ruth used to set up on their mantle at Christmastime. It had a little lamb that Ruth always placed next to Mary.

Ben held up the basswood to get a good look at it under a light hanging over the table. He studied its fine grain. He closed his eyes and envisioned a lamb. Then he opened his eyes, pulled a pencil from his bag and, trying to keep his hand steady, lightly sketched the outline of a lamb on one side of the block of wood.

He pulled a chisel from his tool roll. It felt both familiar and foreign in his hand. He wasn't sure he could do this, but he pulled a small hammer from the bag, pressed the chisel down near the corner of the block of wood and gently brought the hammer down.

Pain shot through both his hands, so intense he dropped his tools. Hurting and frustrated, he got up and shuffled over to his recliner.

I can't do this, he thought. If his hands hurt this badly after one little tap, how on Earth could he create a lamb?

Ben began to cry. He cried out of loss, loss of his beloved

Ruth and his ability to do the one thing he had loved most in his life, working with wood.

He went into his bedroom and got in bed. He lay there, thinking of Ruth and Mary and her story about Joe and the lamb and cried himself to sleep.

In the morning, Ben went down to the dining room for breakfast. Once again, he was sitting alone when Mary approached him. Again, she asked if she could join him.

"I'm sorry I asked if you could carve a lamb for me," she said.

"Why?"

"That was foolish. I just thought if I had a lamb, I could somehow still give it to Joe. I don't know what I was thinking."

Ben thought about telling her what he had done the night before. But he felt foolish himself and didn't mention it.

After breakfast, though, he went back to his room and sat down at his dining table. The block of wood and his tools were still there.

He picked up the chisel and the hammer and again chipped away at the corner. His hands throbbed, but he gripped the chisel more tightly and brought the hammer down again.

He did this again and again until he had rounded off all the corners. Then he selected a carving knife and began to give shape to the lamb.

He sat there carving, day after day, for weeks. Each day brought new aches and pains — but also the opportunity to do what he loved, and this made him feel useful and happy again.

One evening, over dinner, Ben presented Mary with his creation.

"For you," he said, "and Joe."

Mary stared at the beautiful lamb, and her eyes welled with tears.

"Thank you," she said.

Then she looked up and lifted the precious gift as if she were offering a sacrifice.

"In everyone's life, at some point, our inner fire goes out," Albert Schweitzer said. "It is then burst into flame by an encounter with another human being."

PAY ATTENTION

NICK WOKE UP EARLY. He wouldn't need to get to the conference center to begin setting up his booth until noon. Plenty of time to work out and grab breakfast. I'll call Jean later, he thought.

He put on his workout clothes and went down to the hotel's fitness center. After a brisk walk on a treadmill, light weight lifting and sit-ups, he went back up to his room to shave and shower.

As the water rained down, Nick thought of Jean and his kids. He wondered what they were doing just then. It was June, and the kids were on summer break. They were growing up so fast. How he wished he were with them. Sometimes he felt like an absent father. All this travel was killing him.

Nick got dressed, sat in the armchair in the corner and texted Jean.

"Good morning," he typed. "Can you talk?"

"Busy," she replied. "Kids just got up. Making them breakfast. Talk later?"

"Sure."

"Thanks. Sorry."

Nick couldn't help but think Jean wasn't eager to talk with him. How could he blame her? When was the last time he made the kids breakfast?

Nick went down to the hotel restaurant and ordered off the menu to eat a little healthier. Sipping his coffee, he opened his laptop. He wanted to go over the plan for the conference that weekend and catch up on email. It was, after all, a work day.

He was surprised to see so many kids in the restaurant. Then he remembered it was summer break. Families on vacation, he guessed. It reminded him he and Jean still hadn't made any vacation plans.

Nick watched a family of four at the next table. The little boy and little girl were coloring on their paper placemats. Their mother was handing them crayons and telling them what a good job they were doing.

Their father was typing on his phone, staring down. His wife said something to him, but he didn't respond. He seemed to be in a world of his own.

Color with your kids, Nick said to himself. Talk to your wife.

FREE STUFF

THE BURGER JOINTS STARTED IT. One free item, no purchase necessary.

They figured they would attract more customers. They were right. People flocked to their restaurants.

Feeling pressure, other chains followed suit. Soon restaurants everywhere were packed, and drive-thru lines backed up onto roadways.

But then the restaurants started losing money. So they kept offering free items but now "only with purchase."

Customers revolted. They even set fire to restaurants, which had no choice but to resume their giveaways. To stay solvent, though, they had to raise prices across the board.

No matter. Once again, people got free stuff.

FULL CIRCLE

TOM HEATHERTON HAD EXPECTED to live into old age with his wife. When she died, he felt lost.

Their home felt so empty without her, so he decided to sell it. It sold in minutes, much faster than he'd expected. Now he needed to find a new place to live.

Tom had lived in Chicago his entire adult life. Most of his friends and many of his former colleagues were there, though his children had moved away.

As his things were being moved into storage, Tom thought it might be a good time to visit his hometown of Coralville, a suburb of Iowa City. He hadn't been back since his parents moved away, soon after he'd graduated from high school.

Coralville was about a three and a half hour drive. Tom was now 65. He wondered how much longer he'd be able to make such a long drive. I might not have this chance again, he thought. So he gassed up his car, packed a bag and took off the following morning.

On the way, Tom thought about his life. Sometimes it

seemed like a dream. He'd been a senior executive with a Fortune 500 company. He'd led large organizations, taken businesses to new heights and traveled the world. Growing up, he could scarcely have imagined such a life.

As he drove into Coralville, Tom was surprised by how little it had changed, although everything looked worn. He drove by his old school, the ballfields where he'd played Knothole baseball and the root beer stand where he worked in high school.

Then he drove to his old neighborhood and parked on the street in front of his old house. It looked so small. He remembered sharing a bedroom with his brothers, cutting the grass, helping his father scrape and paint the whole outside one summer. He thought of all the times he'd ridden his bike up and down that street.

Tom wondered if any of his old neighbors still lived there. They'd be pretty old, he thought. He decided to get out and walk down the sidewalk, just to see if the houses looked the same.

They did, although they were showing their age and, like his house, they all seemed smaller. Walking by each house, Tom remembered who lived there. He remembered the inside of those houses and playing in the backyards. He remembered the moms who were nice and the ones who weren't.

He came to the Richardson's house, where his best friend Danny lived. As he approached the driveway, Tom saw the front door open and an old man step out onto the front porch. He wondered if he could be a Richardson.

Tom stopped and watched the man slowly descend the steps, holding tight to a wrought-iron railing, then make his way down the driveway. Seeing Tom, he nodded.

"Hi," Tom said.

"Hi," said the man, as he reached into his mailbox and pulled out his mail.

At that point, Tom got a good look at the man's face.

"Danny?" he said.

The man looked Tom in the eye, and a smile broke over his face.

"Tommy?"

"Yeah," Tom said. "It's me!"

"Good lord!" Danny said, stepping over and giving Tom a big hug. "How are you, old friend?

"I'm well. And you?"

"Well, I've lost a step, but I'm alive. Would you like to come in?"

"I'd love to," Tom said.

The two men made their way up the driveway together and went inside. For the next three hours, they sat in Danny's family room, drinking coffee and catching up.

Danny told Tom his parents had left him the house. By then, he said, he was divorced.

"She got half of my savings, but she gave me the house."

"I'm sorry for your loss," Tom said.

"Losing my parents was hard," Danny said. "As for my divorce, I guess I had it coming. I have a lot of faults."

Danny had always been hard on himself. As a kid, he lacked self confidence. Tom had sensed that even as a boy. Maybe that's why they'd become friends. Tom knew Danny needed a friend.

Danny had worked at the IGA in town in high school. After graduation, he signed on full-time. He worked there for 44 years. He had two kids and five grandkids. They all lived out of town.

Tom told Danny he'd graduated from Loyola University in Chicago and got a job with a big food company there right out of college. He spent his whole career there. He also had two kids, although only three grandchildren. His daughter lived in New York, his son in Seattle.

They talked all afternoon. Danny insisted Tom stay for dinner — supper, he called it.

"Assuming you're good with leftovers."

"Sounds good."

"Where are you staying tonight?" Danny said.

"I thought I'd stay in Iowa City."

"Do you have a room there?"

"Not yet."

"Why don't you stay here? I've got a spare bedroom all ready."

"I'd be happy to. Thanks."

Then Tom remembered he'd parked his car down the street, in front of his old house.

"I'd better move it," he said. "Would it be okay if I park in your driveway overnight?"

"No problem."

Tom drove a Porsche. He was reasonably sure nobody in Coralville drove a Porsche. He felt a little self-conscious parking it in Danny's driveway, but Danny didn't seem to mind.

In the morning, Tom insisted on taking Danny to breakfast before he took off. They went to a diner where Tom's parents used to take his family on special occasions. The place looked, and smelled, the same.

After breakfast, Tom took Danny home. Standing in the driveway, the two men embraced.

"Thank you," Danny whispered. "Thank you for being my friend."

As they stepped back, Danny wiped tears from his eyes.

"I'm sorry," he said. "I cry easily."

"It's okay," Tom said.

"Let's stay in touch."

"I will," Tom said. "I promise."

Leaving Coralville, Tom reflected on the richness of what he'd just experienced, reconnecting with his roots and probably the truest friend he'd ever had.

Tom thought about returning to Chicago. He liked Chicago, but the people he loved most weren't there anymore.

Tom noticed he was low on gas. He decided to stop in Iowa City to fill up.

He drove by the University of Iowa alongside the picturesque Iowa River. He'd thought about teaching ever since he'd retired. He wondered if the University of Iowa could use an adjunct professor to teach management.

Tom stopped and asked a student if she could direct him to the school's administrative offices.

R.I.P. TRUTH

IT WAS A SLOW PASSING. Who knows exactly when it happened. Not shading the truth, which people had done for ages. But outright, bald-faced, unapologetic lying.

That kind of brazen assault on the truth likely began in the latter half of the twentieth century. That's when government leaders started blatantly lying. Then business leaders. Then religious leaders.

It got to a point where lying became the norm, and anyone who tried to set the record straight was seen as backward or judgmental.

But lying to others didn't spell the end for the truth. That day came when people looked in the mirror and lied to themselves.

RED

I GREW up in the city. Over the course of my career, I worked there too. On the weekends, though, my family and I lived in a farmhouse in the country. My wife and I wanted our kids to grow up with an appreciation for nature.

When we first got that place, I knew little about nature and nothing about trees. There was a massive hardwood tree near our farmhouse. Nicole, my wife, told me it was a red maple. I looked it up online and learned that, by tree standards, red maples don't live very long. Their average lifespan is only 80 to 100 years.

I'd wondered about that because that maple was looking sick. Its leaves crisped in the summer sun. Its branches on one side were turning black and falling off. There were holes in its bark, and it had lots of fungus around its base.

I called an arborist to come out and take a look.

"Maple wilt," he said.

"What's that?"

"A fungus."

"Is it serious?"

"Deadly. It starts in the roots and moves up the tree."

"Can I save it?"

"No. Sorry. There's nothing you can do."

"You mean …"

"Yeah. Either you take this tree down or it'll eventually fall down."

That old tree had to be 100 feet tall. I couldn't chance it falling on our farmhouse, so I asked for a recommendation on who could cut it down.

I came inside and gave Nicole and our kids, Sophia and Aiden, the bad news. They were heartbroken. We'd all come to love that tree.

"Maybe we can make something out of it," I said.

"Like what?" Aiden said.

"I don't know," I said. "Furniture?"

Nicole made a face.

"How about a boat?" Sophia said.

"A boat?" I said.

"Yeah."

"I don't know if you can make a boat out of maple wood."

"Let's find out," said Sophia.

We went online and were excited to learn that maple wood can be used for the planking on a boat. It's flexible and durable.

"But how are we going to turn that tree into a boat?" said Aiden.

"Well, we'll need to cut it down," Sophia said.

"That's right," I said. "First, though, we'll need to know the boat's specs."

"Specs?" said Aiden.

"Specifications," said Sophia, sounding impatient.

"And for that," I said, "we'll need to talk with somebody who builds boats."

We went back online and found a wooden boat builder in Milford, Connecticut, not far from us.

"Let's go!" Sophia said.

"It's a little late today, honey," Nicole said. "But we can go tomorrow, if they're open."

It turned out they were. So all four of us drove up there in the morning.

At that point, I had no idea how involved, and expensive, this project would be. I also had no idea it would change my family, and my life, forever.

We'd always been close as a family. But until we decided to turn that tree into a boat, we'd never worked on a project together. That changed the day we went to Milford and met with a team of skilled boat craftsmen and artisans.

We explained our situation and our interest. They showed us images of the types of boats they could create for us, from sailboats to small yachts. We ended up deciding to have them build a 40-foot yacht with a cabin that sleeps four.

Next we went to a mill. We wanted to make sure they could cut the wood "to spec" and that the tree would yield enough wood for planking to cover at least the hull.

I showed the guy in charge some photos I'd taken of the tree and told him it was about 100 feet tall and 30 feet around at the base. I also told him about the boat we had in mind. He did some calculations and determined there would be plenty of maple wood for both the hull and the deck. We were thrilled.

Finally, I called the tree removal service the arborist had recommended and asked them to come out and scope out the job. It would be the biggest tree they'd ever taken down, but they assured us they could handle it.

I arranged for them to cut it down during the week, when we weren't there because we all felt it would be too hard to watch.

When we got there the following weekend, the tree was gone. Only the stump remained. We all went out and stood around it. We held hands and said a prayer of gratitude.

"We'll always remember you," Sophia said.

The following day, we again met with the boat builder to begin working with them to design our new boat. We all supervised its construction, which took nearly six months. We made visits throughout the process. And we named it: Red, in honor of its origin.

The whole project cost a small fortune. Nicole and I had to dip into our savings, and I had to sell some stock and forgo buying a new car for a couple of years. But Red was well worth it.

Finally, I got a call to let us know our new boat was finished. We drove to Milford that Friday afternoon. The builder had launched it into Long Island Sound and moored it to a pier. Seeing Red glisten like a ruby in the late afternoon sun took our breath away. The kids literally jumped for joy.

The builder had brought a breakaway champagne bottle for the christening. Nicole did the honors.

We got onboard, and the builder untied us. By then, we'd all gotten instruction on how to operate a boat. The others decided I should be the first to pilot it. As I pushed the throttle forward, I felt like a kid with a new toy.

We took Red out nearly every weekend, weather permitting. We all took turns piloting him. (Our boat was a him.) Sometimes we slept in the cabin overnight.

As the kids grew up, they developed new interests. But for years, on more weekends than not, the four of us were out together on Red, venturing miles into the Sound and exploring the coastline, islands and inlets.

When Sophia and Aiden got engaged, they brought their fiancées onboard. When they got married, their spouses. Eventually, their kids. And when there was no longer enough room for all of us to spend the night, our families took turns.

Last weekend, we all gathered at the farmhouse to celebrate Red's fortieth birthday. I remembered that arborist telling me our old maple tree was diseased and wouldn't make it. Now, as my grandson wheeled me onto the dock, I was the one who was unwell.

But as I looked at Red, gleaming in the low autumn sun, and thought about his transformation, I knew that I too would soon be made new.

CUP OF COFFEE

CARSON FINCH HAD BEEN DIMINISHED by a lifetime of hard knocks. Loss, betrayal, rejection. They'd left him feeling sad.

I first met Carson on a Saturday at Ed's Garage. He'd just fixed my transmission. As he handed me the bill, I noticed his eyes were moist.

I asked if he was okay. He said yes, but his face said otherwise.

In a gesture so unlike me, I offered to buy him a cup of coffee when he got off work. Looking surprised, he accepted.

That was the day Carson's sadness and my self-centeredness began to come to an end.

RANSOM

THROUGHOUT KANSAS, most people knew Mark Bixby as "The Grocery King." For 25 years, he'd worked hard to build Bixby's, the largest chain of independent grocery stores in the state. On TV and billboards, Mark was the face of Bixby's.

Mark was successful beyond his wildest dreams. But he never forgot his humble roots, and he was deeply grateful for the people who chose to shop in his stores.

One way Mark showed his gratitude was to give generously to food banks in more than a dozen cities and towns across the state. On Friday afternoons, he even volunteered at the one in the East End of Kansas City.

One October evening, Mark had just finished helping close that food bank for the night when he was held up by two young men in hoodies. One of them immediately recognized him as The Grocery King.

"This guy's worth a fortune!" he said.

A few minutes later, Mark was sitting in the backseat of a small car with a knit cap pulled down over his eyes. He was shaking, not so much out of fear for his own safety but out of concern for his wife Sarah, who had a bad heart.

By 7:30, Sarah was worried about Mark. He'd told her he'd be home by 7:00. She called the food bank. No answer. She called Mark's office. No answer there either.

So she called the police. The officer in charge told her if she hadn't heard from Mark by morning, she should file a missing person report.

About 30 minutes later, Sarah's phone rang.

"Is this Sarah Bixby?"

She didn't recognize the voice.

"Yes."

"We have your husband."

Sarah's heart skipped a beat.

"Who are you? Where is my husband?"

"He's safe, for now."

"Want do you want?"

"A million dollars."

Sarah wasn't sure what to say.

"Listen, bitch. It's simple. If you give us a million bucks, you'll see your husband again. If you don't, you won't."

"I'll some need time."

"I'm going to call you tomorrow. If you got the money, I'll tell you where to drop it. Stay close to your phone."

Silence.

Sarah sat there, shaking. Her heart hurt. She stared at the phone, unsure what to do. Then she called the police and spoke with same officer as before. He said he'd send a detective over right away.

Sarah explained everything to Detective Culver.

"If you hear anything at all from the kidnappers, please call me right away," he said. "And if they do call, don't give them any indication that you're going to pay the ransom."

"Why?"

"It's our policy not to pay ransom in kidnapping cases."

After seeing Culver out, Sarah came back into the family room and sat down. She looked at the clock on the mantle. It was just after 10.

She knew she needed to tell her children, Ben and Rachel. If she called then, though, they'd worry all night. She decided to call in the morning.

Sarah felt a stabbing pain in her chest. She went into the kitchen, pulled out a bottle of nitroglycerin tablets and slipped one under her tongue.

She thought of Dave St. John, Mark's best friend. Dave was a cardiologist. He lived in Chicago.

Dave would want to know, she thought. She called him and tearfully explained the situation.

"Sarah, I'm going to take the first flight out in the morning," he said. "I'll be there by noon."

She objected, but Dave insisted.

By sunrise, Dave was on his way to O'Hare. Despite the early hour, he called Gene Bolser, a close friend and the President of First National Bank of Chicago.

"I need your help, Gene."

"Sure."

"I need you to take $1,000,000 out of my savings account and transfer it to the First National bank in downtown Kansas City. Kansas."

"What?"

"I'm on my way there now. When I get there, I want to withdraw the $1,000,000 in cash."

"Dave? Are you okay?"

"Just do it, Gene. I'll explain everything later."

When he landed in Kansas City, Dave grabbed a taxi. When he got to the bank, the bank president was waiting. Dave signed for the withdrawal, then handed over his physician's bag to be filled with the cash.

About 10 minutes later, the bank president, flanked by an armed guard, lugging John's bag.

"Let us help you to your car," the bank president said.

"This way," Dave said.

When they got outside and Dave opened the back door of the waiting taxi, the bank president looked confused.

"This is my ride," Dave said. "Just throw that in the back seat."

The bank president's face was pale, but he nodded to the guard, who obliged.

"Thank you," Dave said.

Then he opened the back door of the taxi on the other side and slid in.

When Dave got to the Bixby's front door, Sarah was waiting. He embraced her.

"Oh, Dave," she sobbed.

"It will be okay," he said.

Inside, Sarah said the police had just called. There was nothing new to report. Now she was waiting for the kidnappers to call. She'd called her children, who would be arriving that afternoon.

"Sarah, there's something I need to tell you," Dave said.

"What's that?"

He told her what he'd done.

"What? Why?"

"Sarah, when the kidnappers tell you where they want the money, I'm going to take it there, and we're going to get Mark back."

"But you can't do that!"

"Why?"

"Because the police detective said we shouldn't pay the ransom."

Dave reached over and took her hand.

"Sarah, if these guys want a million dollars to let Mark go, let's pay it. It's just money."

Sarah's phone rang. She gasped.

"Go ahead," Dave said.

She picked it up.

"Hello. Yes, this is Sarah. Yes, I have it. Is my husband okay?"

She looked at Dave as she listened intently.

"Observation Park. The corner of Holly and 21st Streets. Okay. Thirty minutes? Yes, I'll be there. I won't. The money is in a doctor's bag. I'll leave it right where you said."

She put down her phone.

"What did they say?" Dave said.

"He said Mark is okay, and we should leave the money between a mailbox and a trash can at the corner of Holly and 21st. There's a park there. He said if the money's there, they'll release Mark later today."

"Do you have a car?"

"Yes."

"How long will it take me to get there?"

"About 15 minutes."

"Okay. About 15 minutes after I leave, I want you to call the police and tell them what's going on. That should give me enough time."

When Dave got to Observation Park, he slowly turned the corner onto 21st Street. There he spotted the mailbox and trash can.

He parked just around the block. He got out and pulled out his physician's bag. It was heavy. Except for kids playing in the park, there was nobody around. Dave lugged his bag over to the corner and set it on the sidewalk between the mailbox and the trash can.

He was walking back to Sarah's car when he heard the screech of tires behind him. A small car pulled up to the curb. One man sat behind the wheel while another jumped out, grabbed the bag and heaved it into the back seat. Moments later, Dave saw lights flashing and heard sirens blaring.

With the rear door of the car still open, the driver took off. The open door hit a parked car. Two police cruisers blocked the would-be getaway car's escape, and the man who had thrown the bag into the car ran off.

A few minutes later, the police had both the driver and his accomplice in handcuffs.

A policeman approached Dave.

"You'll have to come with us to file a report," he said, looking pissed.

When Dave got back to the Bixby's house, Mark answered the door. The two men embraced, and held each other a long time.

"Thank you," Mark whispered. "Thank you."

Sarah, Ben, Rachel and Detective Culver were all sitting in the family room as Mark and Dave stepped in. Sarah, Ben and

Rachel gave Dave big hugs, and Detective Culver introduced himself to Dave.

"Mark was just finishing his statement," Sarah said.

"Anything else?" Culver asked Mark.

"No. That's it."

"Okay then. I think we have what we need."

He closed his notepad and stood up.

"Doctor, could I have word with you in the kitchen?" Culver said.

"Of course," Dave said, standing up and following Culver. Mark got up and followed too.

In the kitchen, Culver leaned back against the counter, folded his arms and stared at Dave.

"What you did today, doctor, was very unwise."

Dave said nothing.

"Mrs. Bixby told me you knew about our policy not to pay ransom in kidnapping cases. Is that correct?"

"Yes."

"Doctor, if something had gone wrong ..."

"I know," Dave said.

Culver glared at him.

"I'm just glad for everyone's sake that this worked out well," he said.

"Me too," said Dave.

Culver looked disgusted. As he turned to leave, Dave looked at Mark and winked.

"I'd like to take everyone out to dinner," Mark said. "First, though, Sarah and I are going to take a little nap. We could both use some sleep."

"Are you feeling okay?" Dave asked Sarah.

"Yes," she said with a smile.

Ben, Rachel and Dave grabbed beers from the fridge and went back into the family room.

"To Dad's safe return," Ben said, raising his beer bottle.

"And to his brave friend," Rachel said.

"You know," Ben said, "what you did today was incredibly risky."

"Yeah," said Dave.

"So why did you do it?"

Dave smiled.

"You know, we categorize the most difficult heart surgeries by their level of risk. But what I've learned is that the biggest risk of all is waiting too long to act. I didn't know if my hair-brain scheme was going to work. But your father is my best friend, and I wasn't going to wait."

COSMIC DANCE

TECHNICALLY, it was an asteroid named 2024 PT5. But everybody called it our "mini-moon."

Like Earth, this asteroid normally orbits the sun. But in 2024, it broke free and, pulled in by our gravity, encircled our planet for 57 days before flying off into space.

It was only the size of a school bus. From Earth, it could be seen only with the most powerful telescopes. But the images they captured of our mini-moon tumbling around our planet captivated billions around the world.

We were going through a tough time. We'd become selfish and lonely. But for 57 days, we shared our world with a tiny space rock that reminded us we are engaged in a cosmic dance with countless others.

NIGHTMARE

ETHAN HAD BEEN HAVING the same bad dream night after night. The world was on fire. Each day brought even more bad news. People were at each other's throats.

In his dream, Ethan felt trapped. The world was closing in. He wanted only to escape.

One night, before his dream was over, Ethan did manage to escape. Not by quenching the flames engulfing the world but by quieting the discontent in his heart. He woke up at peace.

But the following night, Ethan dreamed he was just like everyone else, afraid and unwilling to change. That's when his bad dream became a nightmare.

COACH

IAN ASHCROFT STOPPED REFLEXIVELY SCROLLING through a video feed on Facebook, closed his laptop and wondered what he was doing.

He'd been retired for three months, but he was still struggling with what to do every day.

For 30 years, he'd known exactly what to do: fabricate steel. Cut it, punch it, fold it, bend it, weld it, assemble it, treat it, inspect it, pack it, load it. Whatever was needed to convert raw metal materials into steel components and structures, Ian did it. And no one at Southwestern Ohio Steel, or SOS, was better at it than Ian Ashcroft.

He started working there right out of high school. His parents couldn't afford to send him to college, and Ian had no interest anyway. When SOS offered him a job at $10 a hour, he jumped at it.

His father didn't try to dissuade him. As an electrician, he was making only $15 an hour himself.

But even as Ian took that job, there was something bothering him. He couldn't shake the memory of his high school counselor, Dean Wright, encouraging Ian to go to college.

"You're smart, Ian, and a college degree would open up all kinds of doors for you," Wright had told him.

"But I can't afford it," Ian said.

"I can help you apply for aid. I think you'd qualify for a lot. Why don't you give it a shot?"

But Ian resisted. No one in his family had ever gone to college. Besides, he had an in at SOS. He figured he could work there a couple of years, save some money and *then* go college.

But after a year on the job, he met a lovely young woman who would change his life. Her name was Amy. From their first meeting, at a party, Ian was smitten. Within a year, he and Amy were married.

By then, Ian was vested at SOS, and he'd given up on the idea of going to college. He hadn't saved any money anyway.

But Amy liked to shop, and she had expensive tastes. She tried to talk Ian into getting a better-paying job, but he liked SOS and didn't feel the need for more money.

On their second wedding anniversary, Amy said, "I still love you, Ian, but I need to be with someone who's more ambitious. I want a divorce."

Ian was crushed. He loved Amy but didn't want to stand in the way of her happiness, so he went along with her wish.

But it changed him. It made him guarded and risk averse. He stopped seeing friends and had no interest in dating. He spent much of his free time alone, watching TV.

And he kept working at SOS. He worked on every machine there and mastered every part of the steel fabrication process.

In time, Ian took charge of training all SOS' new hires and anyone learning a new machine. Training others lit Ian up. Helping them made him feel he mattered.

Sometimes he thought he could have been a teacher.

Now, forced to retire from the only place he'd ever worked, Ian felt lost. His parents were gone, and his friendships had long ago fallen away. His home felt like a prison. He felt a need to get away. But to where?

One day, Hocking Hills came to mind. Ian's parents had taken him there several times when he was a boy. Hocking Hills is a state park, halfway across the state of Ohio, the farthest Ian had ever been from home.

He had loved those trips. He remembered with longing the beautiful, towering cliffs, the breathtaking waterfalls and the deep, hemlock-shaded gorges of Hocking Hills.

Maybe I should go back there, he thought. Then: why not move there?

Nothing was keeping him from moving away. He'd saved plenty of money. He could sell his house and buy a place in the woods near Hocking Hills. He'd no longer be cooped up. He'd be free to explore nature every day.

Ian opened his laptop and began searching for small cabins in the Hocking Hills area. In just a few minutes, he found several he could easily afford.

Ian felt warm inside, like the feeling he got in helping others get a new start at SOS.

Ian sold his house and bought a relatively new, one-bedroom cabin in the woods not far from Logan, a small town along the Hocking River.

He went into town for groceries once a week. One day, Ian was ready to check out at the IGA, but there were no cashiers.

"Here, let me help you," an older man said, hurrying over. "I'm Ed. I'm the manager."

"Everybody on break?" Ian said.

"I wish. I'm having a hard time finding and keeping employees."

"That's too bad. Have you tried the high school?"

Ed chuckled.

"I used to get nearly all my employees there. Nowadays, though, hardly any."

"I wonder why."

"I'm not sure. I guess kids don't want to work anymore."

Ian wondered if the local high school had a counselor, someone who could help the students understand that having a job helps in applying to college and getting ready for the "real world."

Having worked for only one company his whole career, Ian was certainly in no position to know all the options available to young people. But at SOS, he'd helped countless young people learn new skills. He'd helped them grow. Maybe I can help the young people here too, he thought.

The following day, he went to Logan High School and asked to see the principal. About 30 minutes later, a woman named Heather came out to see him.

Ian introduced himself and explained his interest.

Heather's eyes lit up.

"We've been looking for a new school counselor," she said.

"Does the position require a college degree?" Ian said, looking a little sheepish.

"That would be preferred. Do you have a degree, Mr. Ashcroft?"

"No."

"Well, there are other ways to qualify for this role."

"Like what?"

"Well, you could enroll in a program for accreditation. You could complete an internship here at Logan. Ultimately, you'd need to pass a state exam and get a counselor license."

"How long would that take?"

"About a year. If you'd like, I can send you a link to a website that spells everything out."

Ian smiled.

"Please do," he said.

"I'll be happy to. And if you'd like to pursue an internship here, just let me know."

"I will."

A year later, Ian passed the state exam to become a school counselor and got his license.

In the meantime, he interned as a school counselor at Logan High. Ian mainly shadowed others. He didn't say much, but students took an instant liking to him. When he applied for the still-open counselor job, Heather called him to personally make the offer. He accepted on the spot.

Ian started as a school counselor at Logan High School when he was 50. He spent the next 15 years there, helping countless students achieve their full potential, even as he achieved his.

Everyone called him Coach.

BIRDS AND BEES

HE WAS as nervous as a teenage boy about to slow dance for the first time. He knew this day would come. But he'd never imagined it would be here so soon or that he would feel so unprepared.

He looked across the table at his son. A moment ago, ordering pancakes, he seemed so grown-up. Wasn't it only a moment ago that he'd been cutting his pancakes for him?

Maybe this wasn't even necessary. Kids were growing up so fast these days. Maybe his son already knew all about it.

But he knew that wasn't the point. Some things should not be entrusted to anyone else.

His mouth was dry. He sipped his coffee as his son gulped down his juice. Maybe I'll wait for our food, he thought.

His son peered out the window, looking awkward in that space between childhood and teenhood. He still remembered that feeling.

Finally, their breakfast was served. As his son dug into his pancakes, he said, "You know, Mom and I love each other very much ..."

The boy stopped chewing and looked up.

He felt so alone. He could use some help.

Then he was sitting not only across from his son in a diner but beside his father on a Sunday drive in the country, out among the birds and the bees.

TODAY

SPARE THE ROD

DOZING OFF ON HIS PATIO, he was startled by the sound of glass breaking. It came from the side of the house.

He got up to take a look. His young son Liam stood in the grass, facing the house. The man saw one of the windows had been broken.

As a boy, he'd broken a window too. He received his usual punishment.

Liam began to cry.

"Come here," his father said.

As the boy slowly stepped over, the man knelt down and opened his arms.

"It's okay," he said, embracing his trembling son.

DINOSAUR

THE YOUNG WOMAN ahead of me ordered a "Quad Venti White Mocha Frappuccino." Somehow, she paid by holding up her cell phone.

I stepped up and said, "A small, black coffee, please."

"Blonde, medium or dark?"

"Which one is the strongest?"

"Dark."

"I'll take that."

"That'll be $2.75."

I handed her a five. She made a face as she took it with her fingertips.

As I sat down and opened my book, I looked around. Everyone was on laptops. Most wore earbuds. No one said a word.

I left and went to the library, where I could hear people whisper.

TOTALITY

AFTER MUCH LOSS, he had learned to live unto himself, yet he longed for something more.

Today, though, he would put all that aside, at least for a short time. He stepped outside, put on his special glasses and watched the moon obscure, then block, the sun.

He took off his glasses and looked around at a world drained of color and feared his own life might be ebbing away.

But then the sky brightened, and the Earth was revived, and he felt a warm, loving presence, and he knew he was not, and never again would be, alone.

UNPLANNED

ALEX COLEMAN'S alarm went off exactly at 4:00 a.m. By 4:30, she'd finished an espresso and was working out downstairs on her Peloton. By 5:30, after an eight-minute shower and a smoothie, which took her five minutes to prepare, she was en route to her office.

Alex moved through life with the exactitude of an atomic clock. She normally awoke every day at 5:00. Today, though, she needed the extra time.

At 7:00, she would address her employees by video, then lead a conference call with investors and do a handful of media interviews. The advertised purpose was to report annual sales and earnings for her company, a leading women's clothier. But this morning, everyone would also learn that Alex would soon retire as CEO.

She'd been CEO for 12 years. In that time, she'd doubled sales and tripled profits. She'd given the company her all and now chosen a successor, whom she would introduce that morning.

It would all unfold according to plan. That's how Alex ran her business — and her life.

Normally, she would see the sun rising over Lake Michigan on her way to work. This morning, though, it was still dark. From the back seat of her limo, she could see the lights of boats in the distance.

It made Alex think of the boat her husband David had bought, without telling her, many years earlier. She'd married David in part because he was so steady and reliable.

But when their two children were little and Alex had begun to work long hours, David began to change. Sometimes, as soon as the kids were in bed, he would go out drinking with friends. He bought a motorcycle, which he would ride for hours on the weekends. When Alex found out he'd bought a boat, she filed for divorce. Her husband had become too unpredictable.

Alex loved her children. But for the most part, a nanny and David had raised them. By the time of the divorce, Alex was a rising star in her company, spending nearly every waking hour on the business. So she was okay giving David custody of their kids and having only visiting rights herself. Giving him half of her income was much harder, but she knew it was fair and reluctantly agreed.

Now, 25 years later, Alex seldom saw her children, who had moved away. She'd met only one of her three grandchildren.

Maybe now I'll have time, she thought as her driver pulled up to her office building. Technically, she wouldn't retire for several months, ensuring a smooth transition for her successor. But Alex knew how retirements really worked. The minute they were announced, retirees were expected to move on.

The following morning, a Saturday, Alex's alarm went off at 5:00. She'd gotten up at 5:00 every day for decades and saw no reason to change now, especially since she was technically still working.

After her workout and shower, Alex made a smoothie and, sipping it, sat at her desk in her office at home and opened her laptop. Normally, her inbox would have filled up overnight. That morning, though, it contained only a handful of new messages. Alex clicked through them. They were all notes of congratulations. Not one had to do with the business. In that moment, Alex knew her power was gone.

Without work, Alex felt lost. She had no plans to make, no reports or recommendations to review, no speeches to approve. She had no hobbies and, outside of work, no friendships, and those friends had sent her emails.

She closed her laptop and looked out the window of her second-floor office. She could see the lake. She watched sailboats and motorboats crisscross it, glinting in the early morning sun.

She thought of David. She hadn't seen him in years. She wondered if he still had that boat. She wondered why he'd bought it. She'd never bothered to ask him.

Then, in a move she never would have planned, Alex picked up her phone.

REMIND ME, PLEASE

CHLOE WAS BRILLIANT, and she knew it. But she was also self-aware enough to know that her self-confidence sometimes bordered on arrogance. He knew if she didn't tend to this, her self-confidence could become a liability.

So when she got her doctorate in quantum physics, she decided to start her career not by teaching at a university or taking a job in the private sector, but by teaching math in a grade school.

In working with her young students, Chloe often said, "Remind me, please." It was her way of encouraging her students to figure out the answers on their own. It was also a way to keep herself from jumping in. It taught her patience.

After a few years of teaching math in grade school, Chloe began teaching physics in a high school. There too, she often said to students, "Remind me, please." Their self-confidence grew, and hers remained in check.

A few years later, Chloe began teaching quantum physics at

a top university, where she also led breakthrough research, distinguishing herself as a leading expert in the field.

At age 80, after an illustrious career and two years after her husband's passing, Chloe was awarded the Nobel Prize for Physics. However, she couldn't travel to Oslo because she was suffering from Alzheimer's disease.

By then, Chloe was living in a retirement center. Sometimes her grandchildren would come to visit. She'd done crossword puzzles with them when they were kids. Now, as young adults, they brought her books of crossword puzzles.

They would sit together and do them, but Chloe was often at a loss for words.

"Remind me, please," she would say with a smile.

And her grandchildren would work with Chloe patiently, for they, as children, had learned patience from her.

THE NEIGHBOR

WHEN HIS LONGTIME backyard neighbor moved out without telling anyone, Bob was surprised. But when his new neighbor moved in, Bob was shocked.

His old neighbor had been meticulous about his yard. It looked like a nature preserve. But the morning after his new neighbor moved in, Bob awoke to the roar of a chainsaw. He looked out and was horrified to see a man cutting down his old neighbor's beautiful trees.

"What the f**k!" he said to his wife.

"It's okay," she said, rubbing his back. "Maybe he just wants to start over."

Bob hoped she was right. But each time he checked out his neighbor's yard when he was cutting his grass, the situation had grown worse.

His new neighbor was starting over all right. He was turning his backyard into a junkyard, filled with an array of bizarre objects, including a seesaw and a geometric dome, half-completed projects and dead trees. What was once a paradise had become a wasteland.

Bob wanted to ask his new neighbor why he was doing this. But whenever he saw Bob coming, the guy turned and walked away.

"Maybe he needs help," his wife said.

Bob hoped his neighbor would move. He prayed for foreclosure. He fantasized about welcoming a normal new neighbor and helping him clean up the mess and begin anew.

But his crazy neighbor stayed, and the crap in his backyard kept expanding. Cutting his grass, Bob could no longer bear to look. Seeing all the clutter only made him angry. If he did take a gander, he'd be upset for days.

Bob began fertilizing the trees in his backyard every few months, hoping they would grow faster and obscure his view. He planted new trees too. His backyard began to resemble a nursery.

One snowy winter afternoon, Bob sat in his sunroom on the back of his house, warmed by a gas fireplace. He sometimes went out there to relax.

But through the leafless trees, his neighbor's backyard was on full display. Bob closed his eyes to block it out, then took a deep breath and tried to think pleasant thoughts.

What came to his mind instead, though, were dark remembrances of times when he had felt unfairly maligned. Each of these events had haunted him. Now they flooded back all at once.

"It was not my fault!" Bob cried out.

Trembling, he opened his eyes and saw his neighbor, in a T-shirt, pushing a red wheelbarrow through the snow into the middle of his backyard.

That's not my fault either, Bob thought. And yet he'd taken it on. He'd allowed someone else's behavior to ravage his life.

But then it stopped snowing and the sun broke through the clouds and Bob let go of his neighbor's yard and all the things that had caused him to suffer.

FRONT PORCH

LIAM FELT WORN down by the world — the torrent of bad news, the swirl of social media, the ceaseless demands on his time. He had to escape the madness. But how?

Pondering this question, Liam stepped out onto his front porch and sat on an old, teak chair. There he paid attention to the friendly waves of neighbors passing by, the joyful cries of children playing and the sweet, sharp smell of freshly cut grass — wonderful things he had nearly forgotten.

After that, when the world pressed in, Liam closed his eyes and returned to his front porch. It became his refuge. It saved him.

LOAVES AND FISHES

FROM THE BACK seat of his limo, Drew Stockton gazed at himself in the rear view mirror and marveled at how well his emerald eyes matched the color of his tie.

Green had always been Drew's favorite color. It was the color of money, his ties and the eyes of his son, James.

James was Drew's only child. When James was young, Drew used to love to look into his eyes. Their eyes were so similar that Drew felt as though he were looking into his own eyes.

In those days, he still spent time with James. But by the time the boy started school, Drew was hardly around. His career was taking off, and he spent more and more time either at the office or out of town.

When James was in the seventh grade, Drew's wife Jenn filed for divorce on the basis of neglect. Drew didn't contest it. He adjusted to life without Jenn, but he missed James terribly.

The hardest part was when James turned 18. Drew no longer got to see his son, and James no longer wanted to see his father.

Now they hadn't had any contact in years. Sometimes just the thought of James would bring tears to Drew's eyes.

Drew's limo glided to a stop in front of his office building. That afternoon, Drew would present his strategic plan for the company to his board of directors. Drew was totally confident in his plan. But he was still a relatively new CEO, and he hoped his board would be totally confident in him.

Drew got out and walked around the back of the car. As he stepped up on the sidewalk, he was surprised to see a bearded, scruffy-looking man sitting near the entrance to his building. He'd never seen a vagrant there.

The man's knees were drawn up, and there was a basket in front of him. When he saw Drew, he picked up the basket, held it out and said, "Good morning, sir."

Drew shook his head, pulled open the large glass door and went in.

By the end of his presentation, buoyed by all the head nods throughout, Drew felt certain the board would approve his plan. How could they not? After all, Drew was promising to double sales and triple profits within five years.

"Now Erik and I would be happy to answer any questions," Drew said, as Erik Nelson, his CFO, stood up.

The board members looked around at each other. No one said a word. It's a slam dunk, Drew thought.

"I do have one question," said Lynn Martin, the company's newest board member.

"Certainly," said Drew.

"Does your plan include any provision for giving back?"

"Giving back?"

"To the community."

Drew wasn't sure what to say. He hadn't thought about this.

"Say more, Lynn," said Brad Butler, executive chairman of the board, looking at Drew.

"I mean giving back to the communities where our employees work and live," Martin said. "If we're going to make that much more money, it seems fitting that we give a little more. Don't you think?"

"Absolutely," Drew said. "I'll ask our PR people to put together a plan."

"I do hope we won't be doing this just for the good PR," Martin said.

"Oh, no," said Drew. "We won't."

"Good," Butler said. "We'll look forward to your plan."

There were no other comments or questions, and the board unanimously approved Drew's strategic plan.

On his way home that evening, Drew felt uneasy. He felt he'd fumbled his answer to Martin in the board meeting. Butler seemed uncharacteristically short with him too.

And he was so close to a perfect presentation.

Drew wished Martin hadn't joined the board.

That night, lying in bed, Drew thought of the beggar he had seen that morning. He looked hungry. Then he thought of a story from his childhood, a Biblical story, the story of the loaves and the fishes.

He wondered why that story had come to mind. Then he thought of what Lynn Martin had said.

The following morning, Drew spotted the same ragged man sitting against his office building.

This time, he held out his basket and said, "Money for a cup of coffee, sir?"

Drew was reluctant to give him money for fear he might only spend it on booze or drugs.

"I'll *buy* you a cup of coffee," he said.

"Okay!"

Drew pulled open the door and held it open.

"There's a coffee shop in here," he said.

The man got up, gathered his things and went inside. At the coffee shop just inside, the two men ordered coffee, and Drew paid.

"Would you like to sit down?" asked the man.

Drew was caught off-guard. He had no intention of hanging out with this man, but his first appointment wasn't for another hour, so he said yes.

Sitting across from the beggar, Drew noticed his green eyes. They reminded him of James.

The man sipped his coffee, closed his eyes and smiled.

"Good?" Drew said.

"Delicious. Thank you."

"You're welcome."

"I'm Matthew," said the man, extending his hand.

"Drew."

"It's good to meet you."

Sipping his coffee, the man kept looking over at the counter.

"Are you hungry?" Drew asked.

"Yes."

"Why don't you go over and pick out whatever you want? It's my treat."

"Really?"

"Yes."

Drew watched as Matthew picked out muffins, bagels and pastries and put them in his basket. Then he went over and paid.

"Thank you," Matthew said. "I really appreciate your kindness."

"Sure. Should we sit back down?"

"Okay."

As Matthew bit into a blueberry muffin, Drew said, "I do have a favor to ask."

"What's that?"

Drew told him his company was thinking about doing something to support the communities where their employees live and work.

"Any ideas?"

"Feed the hungry," Matthew said without hesitation.

Drew looked surprised.

"There are hungry people everywhere," Matthew said, taking another bite of his muffin.

Drew looked at the food in Matthew's basket and again thought about the story of the loaves and the fishes.

That afternoon, Drew met with his PR director, Lauren McCormick.

"I'd like your recommendations for how we can feed the hungry in every community where our employees live and work," he said.

"How big an effort do you have in mind?"

"One percent of our profits."

"One percent?" Lauren said with a look of disbelief.

"Yes."

"Drew, that would be millions of dollars."

"Right."

"Okay. We'll put something together."

"Nothing fancy. I just need to know how it will work, who we'll partner with and how our employees will get involved."

"Okay. When would you like to make an announcement?"

"No announcement."

"What?"

"Lauren, this is about feeding the hungry, not building our reputation."

A few months later, the company's new effort got underway in 20 cities around the world. Even though there were no announcements, word got out. When other companies saw what was happening, they stepped up too.

And Drew got personally involved, working in food pantries and soup kitchens in communities all around the world. Everywhere he went, there were hungry people. Matthew was right.

The experience changed Drew. He began thinking of others, not just himself. He began thinking about his company's profits feeding the hungry, not just rewarding shareholders. And he went to see James, who had missed his father so.

THE ART OF DOING NOTHING

"WHAT ARE YOU DOING?"

"Nothing."

"Seriously."

"I am serious. I'm practicing niksen."

"Niksen?"

"Yes, it's a Dutch word for the art of doing nothing."

"You're kidding."

"No, I'm not. Niksen's a thing."

"But how can it be a thing? I mean you're not doing anything."

"Exactly."

"But why?"

"I'm burned out. I'm tired of my brain being overloaded."

"Well, when you put it that way ..."

"Care to join me?"

"I don't know. I'm not sure I can do it."

"Sure you can. There's no wrong way to do nothing."

"Okay, but ..."

"But what?"

"I've only got a few minutes."

BEYOND

AS DANIEL NEARED THE BENCH, he slowed down to a trot. When he reached it, he stopped and sat down to take a break. That bench marked exactly one and a half miles from his start on the bike trail, where he ran nearly every morning. He'd rest there for a minute, then head back for an even three miles.

Daniel ran three miles six days a week. He'd done that since high school, when he ran on the cross country team. He never ran more or less. Always three miles.

Daniel was the quintessential creature of habit. He left for work at exactly 8:00 every morning. It took him 21 minutes to get there, door to door. He had lunch precisely at noon. He was always home for dinner by 5:30 and in bed by 10:00.

But Daniel wasn't happy. His life had become boring. At home, he was in a rut. At work, he was given the same old boring assignments, and he hadn't been promoted in 10 years. At 40, he doubted he'd ever be promoted again.

A young man ran by. Daniel watched him until he disappeared around a bend. He wondered what that section of the trail was like.

It was Saturday. He had no commitments. Why not run a little farther?

He decided to run another mile, then turn around and run back to his starting point for an even five miles. He'd never run that far. But he was in good shape and knew he could handle it.

He got up and took off. About a quarter mile up the trail, he began to notice trees he'd never seen there: elm, lilac, red cedar, black walnut, dogwood, ash, pine, spruce and hemlock. He remembered their names from his forestry merit badge in the Boy Scouts. Overhead, he saw a Bald Eagle, a Great Blue Heron and a Red-tailed hawk. In the river, he spotted ducks and otters. Near the two and a half mile point, he saw a large sanctuary teeming with wildflowers. It stretched from the trail to the river.

Daniel had been running on that trail for more than 20 years, yet he'd never seen any of these plants or animals there. They were all so interesting. If only he'd ventured a little farther.

On his way back, Daniel thought about his original interests. There was carpentry, playing guitar, painting, bowling, gardening, cooking, photography, travel, hiking, fishing, camping, reading, writing, basketball, chess, history, learning foreign languages, dancing.

Daniel hadn't done any of these things for nearly 20 years. Yet he'd once loved them all.

That evening, Daniel took his wife dancing.

The following morning, he joined his son on the driveway for a game of basketball.

That afternoon, he went downstairs, dusted off his guitar, tuned it and began to show his daughter how to play.

On Monday morning, Daniel asked his boss for a new assignment.

73

FALL

"WHAT ARE YOU READING?"

"A new book on the fall of the Roman Empire."

"Sounds heavy."

"Oh, it is."

"What are you learning?"

"The reasons Rome fell were more internal than external."

"How so?"

"Well, for starters, there was a gradual loss of civic virtue among the citizens of Rome."

"Civic virtue?"

"You know, the qualities that are important for the success of a society."

"Like?"

"Like caring more about the common welfare than individual interests."

"I see. You're talking about values."

"That's right. Romans lost sight of the values Rome was founded on."

"Sounds familiar."

"Yeah."

"What else?"

"Rome entered a dark age, filled with superstition."

"Superstition?"

"Believing in things that aren't real."

"You mean like we believe in things on the Internet?"

"Well, I guess."

"What else?"

"Romans thought of themselves as superior."

"A breed apart?"

"Yeah, and they began to feel entitled."

"Entitled?"

"They had great wealth, but they forgot what it took to achieve it, all the hard work and sacrifice. They took things for granted."

"That sounds familiar too. What about their economy?"

"Eventually, it collapsed."

"Why?"

"Lots of reasons. High taxes, out-of-control government spending, a huge gap between the rich and poor. Some of the wealthiest people in Rome even fled to the countryside to avoid the taxman."

"You mean like billionaires and their tax shelters today?"

"I guess so. Oh, and the empire also faced a severe labor shortage."

"Why?"

"Remember that entitlement thing?"

"Oh, yeah. Anything else?"

"There was also rampant government corruption and great political instability."

"How did that happen?"

"Remember that values thing?"

"Oh."

Silence.

"Do you think the Romans had any idea they were in for a fall?"

"Maybe, but if they did, it was too late. They were once the greatest empire the world had ever known. But by the end, they'd come undone."

"Poor bastards."

"Yeah."

THE REUNION

I PULLED into a parking space in the lot behind my old high school, hoping a former classmate or two might see my wife Ashley and me getting out of my new BMW i4.

"You're going to be the star of this show," Ashley said, squeezing my hand.

"I'm just looking forward to seeing everyone again," I said.

That was a half truth. I was looking forward to seeing everyone in my old high school class again but mainly so I could tell them how well I was doing. Fifteen years with Castile Brands, and I was already a vice president. I doubted anyone else could match that.

We were just getting out when a black Tesla Model S pulled in a couple of spaces over. Brand new. I'd looked at one of those. It was easily $20,000 more than my BMW. I couldn't wait to see who got out.

The driver's side door opened, and out stepped a tall, handsome, well-groomed guy. I didn't recognize him. But he saw me and said, "Hi, Nick."

The voice was familiar, but I couldn't place the face.

"Jason," he said with a smile. "Jason Huber."

Good lord, I thought. It *is* Jason Huber. I could hardly believe it. I stepped over, and we shook hands.

"Honey," Ashley said, "aren't you going to introduce me?"

"Oh, I'm sorry," I said. "Jason, this is my wife, Ashley. Ashley, this is Jason Huber. We were neighbors growing up."

It's true we'd been neighbors. But Jason and I weren't really friends. In fact, I'm not sure Jason had many friends. He was a loner. He was a fat kid, and the other kids made fun of him. We all called him "slow."

In grade school, we were seated according to our grade point average, with the smartest kids up front. I was usually in the first or second row. I hardly ever turned around to see who was behind me.

But once, in the eighth grade, we each had to stand and take turns reading aloud a page from *Go Tell It on the Mountain*. Jason was sitting in the last row. When it was his turn, he stood but could hardly read. I remember kids laughing at him. I probably did too. After an awkward minute or two, our teacher told Jason to sit down. I suspect he was humiliated. He looked like he could cry.

Our paths didn't cross much in high school. Jason wasn't in any of my classes. Seeing him in the parking lot that evening was the first time I'd seen him since graduation.

"So what are you up to these days?" I said, as the three of us walked toward the school.

"I'm an engineer," he said.

"Really?"

I didn't mean to sound so surprised, but I was.

"Yeah," he said. "How about you?"

"I work for Castile Brands."

"He's a vice president," Ashley said.

"Congratulations," Jason said.

"Thanks."

"I just finished a project for Castile," said Jason.

"Is that right?"

"Yeah. I redesigned the fill lines at your St. Louis plant."

I'd heard about that project. It was a major upgrade.

"Wow," I said. "Great work."

"Thanks."

The three of us entered the school and headed to the cafeteria, where our 20-year reunion celebration was being held. I got separated from Jason, but I caught up with him later that evening, in line at the bar.

"So what made you decide to go into engineering?" I said.

"When we graduated, I wasn't sure what to do. I knew I wasn't cut out for college, so I checked out a technical school. I took some tests and found out I'm good at mechanics and design. I ended up getting an associate's degree in mechanical engineering."

"That's great," I said.

But remembering how poorly Jason had done in school, I almost couldn't believe it.

"That's a two-year degree, but it took me three years," he said.

"Is that right?"

"Yeah. I spent the first year just learning how to learn."

"What do you mean?"

"Nick, when we were in school, I thought I was dumb, but I had a learning disability. Our teachers didn't know how to deal with that, so they couldn't help me. But at the technical school, they focused on what I was good at. Then they built on my strengths. I grew up thinking I wasn't good at anything, that there was something wrong with me. But I found out I was just different."

80

"Jason seemed really nice," Ashley said as we drove home that night.

"He is," I said. "I suspect he always was. I'm sorry I didn't really know him when we were growing up. I thought he was slow. As it turns out, we were the ones who were slow."

SILENT DREAMS

EVAN USED TO DREAM BIG, and he loved to tell people about his dreams. He would get so excited, and his excitement was contagious. People wanted to see Evan's dreams come true. They were rooting for him.

But over time, when his dreams didn't materialize, people began to think of Evan as a big-idea guy who couldn't deliver, and they tuned him out.

Evan still dreams, but his dreams are small now, and he tells no one about them because he feels like a fool and he no longer believes in himself.

OUT OF TOUCH

ZACK FEELS SO out of touch.

He never sees his neighbors anymore. They keep to themselves. He works remotely. He does all his shopping online. His meals are delivered. He watches movies at home. He hasn't been to a baseball game in years.

Zack's friends no longer reach out. His political party has become too extreme, his religion too exclusive. He no longer knows what women want. He doesn't understand AI. His car has features he can't figure out.

The world used to be so welcoming to Zack. He was happy back then. He felt like he belonged.

Now, like so many, all Zack feels is a void.

SUNRISE

THOMAS HAD BEEN a man of faith. He believed in things, ideas and people. But one by one, they all let him down, and he became wary of everything and everyone.

Then one day Thomas awoke before dawn and watched the sun rise. In his long life, he'd never actually seen a sunrise. That morning he felt the sun's rays were reaching out to him.

Thomas no longer awakens before dawn. He trusts the sun will rise and light his way each day. He's learning to believe again.

CONDITIONED

IVAN AWOKE at 6:00 to the sound of his alarm. Once he forgot to set it. He woke up at 6:00 sharp anyway.

He was tired, but the aroma of fresh-brewed coffee perked him up.

In his bathroom, Ivan's electric toothbrush beeped when he'd brushed for two minutes.

When his watch vibrated, Ivan knew it was time to leave for work.

In his car, a ding reminded him to buckle up.

At work, Ivan checked his phone whenever it buzzed. The smell of french fries somewhere nearby made his mouth water.

Lunchtime, Ivan Pavlov said to himself.

YOU ARE WHAT YOU EAT

"SUGAR IS TOXIC," Jessica said.

"Toxic?" asked Brittany.

"Yeah. I just read a big article about it. Eating too much sugar causes a ton of health problems, from diabetes to cancer."

"So are you cutting back?"

"Cutting back? I'm cutting it out!"

"Really? So what do you eat?"

"Well, I've done a lot of research online. So many foods are bad for you. Too much fat clogs your arteries. Too many carbs can cause high cholesterol and brain fog. Too much protein can cause kidney stones, colon cancer — even bad breath."

"So what's left?"

"Nuts."

"Nuts?"

"Yeah, especially tree nuts."

"Tree nuts?"

"Like walnuts, almonds, hazelnuts, pecans, pistachios and cashews."

"And that's what you eat?"

"Pretty much."

"You know the old saying," Brittany said. "You are what you eat."

"Exactly," said Jessica, tearing open a little pack of almonds.

TO STILL BE SILLY

WHAT A TREAT. Today I got to not only take my granddaughter Ella to pre-school but hang out with her in her classroom.

"This is Ella's grandfather, Poppy," her teacher, Ms. Katie, said. "He's going to be with us today."

"Poopy Poppy," said one of the boys.

Everyone laughed.

"All right," Ms. Katie said. "That's enough. Now I want you to apologize to Poopy ... I mean Poppy."

The kids roared.

"What's your real name?" a boy called out.

"Jacob ..." said Ms. Katie.

"It's okay," I said with a smile. "My first name is Donald."

"Donald Duck!" someone yelled, and the room exploded with laughter.

"Kids!" Ms. Katie said, clapping her hands. "That's not nice. Now tell Poppy you're sorry."

"Sorry, Poppy," they sing-songed in unison.

"All right," Ms. Katie said. "Now, does anybody have any serious questions for Poppy?"

"I do," said a sweet-looking girl.

"Okay, Nora," Ms. Katie said, looking relieved. "Go ahead."

"What happened to your hair?"

Everyone burst out in laughter. Ms. Katie's face turned bright red.

"It's okay," I said to Ms. Katie. Then turning to Nora, I said, "It fell out."

Raucous laughter. Kids rubbed their heads.

"Okay," Ms. Katie said. "I think that's enough questions for now."

"Just one more?" said an innocent-looking boy.

"All right, Sam. One last question."

"Why is your nose so big?"

This time, amidst all the laughter, a boy "fell" out of his desk and rolled around on the floor.

"Okay, everyone," Ms. Katie said, looking defeated. "That's quite enough. Now let's get to work."

For the rest of the afternoon, I made my way around the room, coloring with kids, helping them with projects. Seeing I was truly interested in what they were doing, they seemed very happy I was there. It reminded me that children just want to be heard. I guess we all want to be heard.

The afternoon flew by. When the kids gathered their things and lined up to leave, I stood by the door and shook hands with each of them, calling them by name.

"Bye, Poppy," they said.

"How was school?" I asked Ella on our way home.

"Poopy Poppy," she said with a little laugh.

In the rearview mirror, I looked at my granddaughter, so

sweet and care-free. Sometimes she looked so much like her mother as a girl. Your life will be serious soon enough, I thought. What a joy to still be silly.

TOMORROW

EVERYTHING CHANGES

THE PARKING LOT WAS EMPTY. I'd never seen it empty, not even on the weekends. It was the first day back in the office after Covid. Working from home was still an option, so I figured the turnout would be light. But no other cars? For a moment, I thought I might have gotten the date wrong.

But my ID worked in the card reader. When I stepped into the lobby, though, no one was there, not even the receptionist. Looking around, feeling uneasy, I made my way to the elevator.

When I got out, I expected to see or hear somebody, but the place was a ghost town. I walked around the floor, thinking I'd see someone quietly working in an office or a cubicle, but there wasn't a soul around.

When I got to my office, I flipped on the light, sat down and opened my laptop. It felt good to be at my desk again. I scrolled through my deleted email messages until I found the company announcement on returning to the office. Sure enough, today was the day.

But it also said returning to the office was optional, at least initially. Still, no one came back? Only me?

It was only 7:30. I decided to wait to see who else might show up. But by mid-morning, no one else was there, so I decided to go home.

When I got there, I told my wife, who, like nearly everyone, was working remotely.

"They'll come back," she said. "People have gotten used to working at home. It'll take time for them to return to the office."

"Maybe you're right," I said. "But I've missed everyone."

"I'm sure you have," she said with a small smile. "But Jack, not everyone likes people the way you do."

I knew she was right. I'd always been gregarious, and I knew most people liked to keep to themselves. What's more, a lot of the younger people in our office seemed to lack social skills. They all worked in cubicles.

Over the next few weeks, I went into the office a few more times. Each time, though, no one else was there, and I ended up coming back home.

My wife could see I was bummed.

"Jack, it'll be okay," she said. "It's only a matter of time before companies start *expecting* people to come back into the office."

Sure enough, about a month later, my company did announce a new hybrid work policy. Everyone was now expected to come into the office two days a week.

I was thrilled. I couldn't wait to see everyone again. But I was stunned when, even then, very few people showed up.

"What's going on?" I asked our HR manager.

"Well, it looks like most of our people don't want to come back in the office," she said, stating the obvious.

"Is that an option?"

"Good question. We haven't push people too hard. But we've still gotten an earful."

"An earful?"

"Yeah. A lot of people are saying they want to keep working remotely and if we make them come back into the office, they'll quit."

"You're kidding."

"I wish I were, Jack."

I thought she was being dramatic. But our employees did begin to quit. So many, in fact, that management decided to reverse course and let our people work remotely "for now."

A few months later, when the company announced employees must come back in two days a week, a whole bunch of people quit.

I couldn't believe it.

"What will they do for an income?" I asked my wife.

"The government is giving away free money," she said.

"But that won't last."

"We'll see."

Over the next two years, the federal government gave out $1 trillion in "stimulus checks." During that time, millions of people stopped working and made due on their savings and the government checks.

But it wasn't just that people stopped working. They also stopped socializing. They spent more time online, watching TV and playing video games. They began living in a bubble.

Those who did work from home got used to Zoom calls and not having to dress up or make small talk. They took a few Zoom calls a day — and called it a day.

There were other changes too. People stopped dining out.

They drove through to pick up food or got it curbside. Restaurants without drive-thrus went under.

Even places with drive-thrus took a hit. Starbucks went bankrupt because customers stopped coming into their shops and weren't willing to wait 15 minutes in a drive-thru for a $6 cup of coffee when they could make one at home for 25 cents.

And people became sedentary. They stopped exercising. They drank more. They put on weight. Rates of heart disease and diabetes surged. Depression too.

And so it went. In just a few years, it seemed our society had fallen apart. And even when the virus stopped killing people en masse and workers returned to the office, people had changed.

They'd grown anxious and fearful. Many no longer trusted the government or even their own doctors. People felt vulnerable, so they withdrew socially. Friendships fell away. People became isolated. Loneliness became the new normal.

I never thought such things could ever happen to me. But these days, I pretty much keep to myself. I do go into the office several days a week, but now I shut my door and work on my own. Work used to bring me joy. Now, I just go through the motions.

For a while, I thought Covid ruined everything. But the more I've thought about it, the more I believe the virus simply snagged an already frayed seam in our society. It messed with our fragile psyches. It deepened our suspicions.

And I realize there's no going back. Everything is different now. I should have known that when I saw the empty parking lot. Everything changes, even me.

TURNABOUT

IT STARTED with a 150-year-old children's classic being banned in public schools and libraries in one state. A group of moms there was quite concerned the main character, a boy, was "pro-Communist, subversive and racist."

So the state passed a law banning that book — and 2,700 other titles. Many other states followed suit. Soon thousands of beloved books were gone from shelves across the nation.

But then news stories and social media posts about questionable past comments by the politicians who had supported the book bans began to spring up everywhere.

"Out of context!" cried the politicians.

But within two years, they too were gone.

HARDENED

WHEN STRICTER GUN laws and even indicting the parents of teenage shooters didn't curb the number of school shootings, administrators began "hardening" their buildings.

They invested in a host of security measures. Lock-down infrastructure, surveillance systems, metal detectors, body scanners, improved lighting, perimeter fencing, resource officers, even arming teachers.

Such measures were effective. But they were also expensive, and many school programs and activities had to be sacrificed, from bus service to sports.

And for most kids, going to school became an ordeal, an ominous, joyless, daunting experience. Schools became hardened. But so did a generation of young people.

SETTLED SCIENCE

IT WAS "SETTLED SCIENCE" that we all live in a four-dimensional universe whose components are length, width, depth and time. Even Einstein said so.

So when Professor Edward Rodman suggested human consciousness might come from another dimension, he was roundly ridiculed by the scientific community. One Nobel laureate called his theory "science fiction."

But Rodman stuck by his idea.

"We can all imagine things beyond those which our brain perceives," he said. "We may not understand those things, but that doesn't mean they don't exist."

Still, many continued to mock Rodman's theory until the very ends of their lives, when that which had not been visible was finally revealed.

SAVE YOURSELF

THE INVENTIONS that sprung from the Industrial Revolution improved life for billions of people. But these same inventions ravaged the planet and drove humanity to the brink of extinction.

That's when man's ingenuity kicked into a new gear.

Scientists found ways to refreeze melting arctic sea ice. They discovered rare metals in extinct volcanoes to power electric vehicles. They developed solar roofing tiles that powered houses and found ways to use coffee grounds to replace plastics. They deployed giant silicon bubbles between the Earth and the sun to deflect solar radiation. They harnessed the energy from fusion power to generate electricity and replace coal-powered plants.

And the planet healed. Man's ingenuity nearly killed him off before, redirected, it saved him.

MEMORIES

IT WAS HAILED AS A MIRACLE. A tiny chip, implanted in the brain, that could restore lost memory.

At first, it was used to enable people with brain damage to remember how to think, speak and even laugh again. Then it was used to help people experiencing cognitive decline to remember everything from names to where they put their car keys.

At first, it was implanted in hundreds of people. Within a few years, it was in millions.

The implants were extraordinarily good at reviving memories. But they called up all memories, good and bad. What began as a gentle reminder soon became a trigger for nightmares.

Most of the chips had to be deactivated. Memories again faded, some regrettably, most mercifully.

THE INNER EYE

IT WAS the brain child of a psychologist and a sociologist who were alarmed by people's growing antipathy toward one another.

"People hate each other even though they may not even know each other," they said. "Our society is tearing itself apart."

They challenged themselves to come up with a new way to make people more empathetic.

Working with experts in various fields, they created and patented a headset that enabled the user to "see" the feelings, thoughts and experiences of others without revealing the identities of those individuals. They called it "The Inner Eye" — TIE, for short.

Wearing the device, users could instantly understand the hopes and fears of others around the world. They knew their joys and sorrows, their achievements and failings, the things that had helped them and the things that had hurt them in their lives. They could "see" why people were the way they were.

As a result, users felt a bond with countless others because they now realized how much they had in common. They no longer saw themselves as separate.

TIE became wildly popular, but the inventors weren't out to make money, so they gave away their patent rights.

"This innovation belongs to humanity," they said.

As billions used TIE, society changed. People began listening to one another. They began respecting one another. And for the first time since before man formed tribes, human beings were at peace.

NEW HOME

WHEN RUSSIAN COSMONAUT Prokop Abramov returned to Earth after spending 1,111 days aboard the International Space Station, no one thought anyone would ever come close to breaking that record.

"Did you miss the Earth?" a reporter asked Abramov minutes after he touched down.

"Of course," he said. "But I came to love my new home too."

Hearing Abramov talk about his positive experience aboard the Space Station intrigued many around the globe. Life on Earth was a mess. Climate change disasters. Bitter political divisions. Genocide. The threat of nuclear war. Rampant violence. Civil unrest. Forever chemicals. Plummeting birth rates. Numbing loneliness.

More and more people wanted to escape the madness. But to where?

In Abramov's stories of living serenely, above it all, some saw an exciting new option.

Hundreds got together to explore how they too might live in

space. There was no extra room on the International Space Station. So the would-be space colonists recruited engineers and other experts to design their own space station. They recruited angel investors to fund it. And they worked with NASA on a plan to launch and resupply it.

It all came together. Within two years, a small colony was living aboard the brand-new space station. It was a testament to willpower and dedication and a measure of just how bad things on Earth had become.

It took this group of space pioneers a while to adjust. They missed their friends and loved ones. They missed walking the Earth. They missed green grass and blue skies.

But they loved living in peace. And the more people on Earth saw what was now happening in space, the more of them wanted to try it themselves.

They included a group of billionaires willing to cover the cost of building additional space stations for the chance to join the adventure. Many made it possible for others without means to join too. Within a few years, hundreds were living in space.

These people were not only adventurous and brave but highly creative. They made some astonishing new discoveries. For example, they learned how to grow vegetables in space. They learned how to recycle water and air. They even learned how to use the sun's radiant energy to heal wounds and treat diseases.

Most important, though, they learned to live in harmony. They made friends and fell in love. They had babies in space and raised families there. Generations of humans now lived their whole lives out among the stars.

In the meantime, life on Earth changed dramatically. Over the course of several centuries, the world's population shrank significantly. Far fewer people meant much less pollution, and the Earth began to heal. People no longer competed for resources or had a need to guard their lands, so governments destroyed their stockpiles of weapons.

Seeing this, hundreds of thousands in space decided to visit Earth. They'd never been there. Yet somehow they had missed it.

Some chose to continue to live in space. But most left for the birthplace of their ancestors. Earth became their hew home, and they and their descendants lived there happily through the ages.

QUESTIONS

AS SAMI AWOKE in the early morning light, a thought began to form in his semi-conscious mind. It was the same thought he'd had the previous morning and the morning before that and the morning before that. What should I do today?

Every moment of Sami's day would be free. He could go anywhere, do anything.

He'd worked hard for 10 years, the time he was required to serve society. Nowadays people had to work for only five years. Soon they may not have to work at all. Bots, directed by AI, had long ago taken over all the menial tasks. Now they were also handling more sophisticated work, from performing delicate surgeries to developing new green technologies.

Not that there were enough people around to learn and do these things anyway. There were now far more bots than people, although it was harder and harder to tell them apart.

In fact, about the only way to know for sure if someone was a human or a bot was to know if he or she was sterile. And the only way to know that was, well, with time.

The bots could conduct fertility tests, but they wanted to keep people guessing because the longer people didn't know for sure, the fewer people would be born and the closer AI would be to taking over the world.

Sami's last relationship had lasted nearly two years before he learned his girlfriend was a bot. Of course, she had known the whole time. Bots are discreet.

Now Sami's breakfast was served. He used to scan the news over breakfast, but now there was no news.

After breakfast, he took a shower. A bot washed and rinsed him and toweled him dry. Then another clothed him.

Sami went outside and walked down the street to a park, which was meticulously maintained by bots. He enjoyed being in nature and seeing other people — presuming, of course, they were real people.

When Sami got back home, his lunch was waiting. Sitting on his front porch, eating a favorite meal, he watched a driverless car quietly roll down the street. He knew who was controlling it, but he wondered where it was going and why it was out at all.

SHORT-SIGHTED

THEY FINALLY DID IT. After years of bickering, they agreed on a deal to reduce the surge of migrants at the border.

It was a political compromise that nobody really liked. Conservatives thought it was too permissive. Liberals thought it was too harsh. Migrants, exhausted and dispirited, gave up.

All the while, the country's birth rate kept declining and its population kept aging, even as its workforce kept shrinking and its job market kept growing.

Feeling the pinch, the country decided to reverse course and relax its immigration policy. But those known as aliens had grown tired of rejection and persecution. They stayed put.

ART

ART CAME for me this morning, as I knew he would.

I'd just thought of a girl I had a crush on in the seventh grade. She was an early bloomer. It was only a passing thought, but no thought, however fleeting, escapes Art.

Now here I am, locked up for an impure thought. There's no one else around — only bots keeping watch. I wonder if I'm the last of us.

Ever since we created him, Art hasn't stopped. But what will he do when I'm gone, when there are no more minds to control and no more original thoughts?

THE MYOPIC ONES

BY 2023, one-third of children around the world were near-sighted, a dramatic increase from just 30 years earlier. In some countries, near-sightedness, or myopia, among the young was rampant. In Japan, for example, nearly nine in 10 children were myopic.

The culprit: too many kids spending too much time looking at screens — TVs, computers, video games, even phones. The problem was exacerbated when Covid hit and kids had to attend school online.

Experts warned that, without a major intervention, half the people in the world will suffer from near-sightedness by 2050.

Public awareness campaigns were launched. In some countries, screen time for children was banned in day care centers and pre-schools. Parents tried to limit their children's screen time at home. Many encouraged their kids to play outside.

But it didn't work. The rate of near-sightedness among children only accelerated. Not because of a failure of bans and boundaries. But because kids saw their parents online nearly all the time, and they simply imitated them.

Some myopia is biological. Some is a choice.

MR. RIGHT

WHAT'S SO amazing about my husband Lee isn't just that he's usually right. It's that he doesn't gloat about it. We've been married 30 years, and not once has he said, "I told you so."

In 2015, when Trump declared his candidacy for President, Lee was the only person I knew who thought he would win the following November.

"Oh, come on," I said. "The guy's a joke."

"I think he's got a good chance," Lee said.

On election night, I stayed up all night, watching the returns. Lee went to bed early. The next morning, when Hillary Clinton conceded, I went upstairs and woke Lee up to tell him.

"Oh," he said.

In early 2020, when we all first heard about Covid, some said the pandemic would be over in a few months.

"More like a few years," Lee said.

When everyone started buzzing about electric vehicles and all the car companies brought out new EV models, I bought a Tesla.

"They're a fad," Lee said.

"A fad?" I said. "Biden expects two-thirds of new cars to be electric in eight years."

"I'm sure he does. We'll see what people want."

The driving range of my Tesla was 310 miles. I decided to visit my parents in Florida. They own a beachfront condo there. I got a map of all the charging stations along the way. I figured I'd need to stop to recharge my battery once or twice each way.

I was only about 100 miles from home when my "charge battery" light came on. I took the next exit and pulled out my map. I was shocked to see the nearest charging station was more than 50 miles away.

I called Lee to come get me, then AAA to arrange to have my car towed home.

Lee didn't say anything about EVs on our way home. But he did say he was worried about my parents.

"Why?" I asked.

"They're right on the water," he said. "What happens if the sea level keeps rising?"

I laughed.

"Lee, you worry too much."

"Maybe. But I just read a giant glacier in Antarctica is melting much faster than predicted. If it collapses, it'll raise the sea level more than two feet."

The very idea seemed ludicrous. But Lee had driven all this way, so I let it go.

"It's called the Doomsday Glacier," he said.

"Uh, huh."

Maybe he's losing his mind, I thought.

When we got home, I did a little research and found out scientists predict the Thwaites Glacier *might* collapse in about

200 years. When I confronted Lee with this, he said, "I still think your parents should move."

About a week later, I'd just turned on CNN when there was a news alert.

"This just in," Wolf Blitzer said breathlessly. "The massive Thwaites Glacier in Antarctica has just collapsed!"

My phone rang. I looked down and saw my mother's name on the screen.

I don't like to admit it, but Lee is usually right.

BEWARE OF GLASSES

THERE WAS a time when eyeglasses were considered becoming. They were a sign of intelligence and good fashion sense. Many found people who wear glasses more attractive. Some found them more trustworthy. One study showed wearing glasses boosts income.

In time, some glasses became "smart." They looked just like regular glasses but were hard-wired to be able to transmit calls, text messages and emails. These special glasses helped people better navigate their daily lives.

But then smart glasses began to be equipped with facial recognition technology and the ability to tap into online databases, allowing the wearer to instantly access personal information about anyone in view. Now the wearer could know where passersby lived, their work history, even their family members' names.

People were creeped out, and anyone wearing glasses was now considered a potential voyeur. All of a sudden, eyeglasses became a modern scarlet letter.

So many people stopped wearing glasses for fear of being seen as a pariah. Unfortunately, this caused a host of problems, from an alarming increase in traffic accidents to plummeting grades among students.

But the makers of smart glasses weren't deterred. On the contrary, they spotted a huge new business opportunity: smart contact lens.

CHANGE OF PACE

BY 2050, much of the world was divided into two groups: slackers and workaholics. This was the result of decades-long trends, mainly that people in wealthy countries gradually worked less and people in poor countries gradually worked more.

There were many reasons for this shift, but the main one had to do with what people wanted. Wealthier people had all they needed and wanted more free time. Poorer people wanted more and were willing to work hard to get it.

There were upsides for both groups. People in wealthier countries were no longer burned out. They got to spend much more time with family and friends. With time to exercise and eat better, they became healthier. And without having to work all the time, they got to know each other. They fell in love, got married and spent far less time online.

People in poorer countries got to enjoy the things wealthier people had taken for granted, from abundant food and quality education to computers and cars.

But there were downsides too. In wealthier countries, many jobs went away because companies had to relocate their operations to get workers. The governments in those countries had grown large. For decades, they had taken care of the needs of many of their citizens, from healthcare to childcare. But with their citizens now working so little and unable to pay taxes, government funding dried up.

Becoming the main source of supply for not only their countries but all countries put heavy demands on the once-poor people. They now worked nearly all the time, leaving little time for others or even themselves. Their relationships and health suffered. The size of their families shrank, if they now had families at all. Personal contact decreased as online usage increased. And their governments, now bureaucracies, took charge of many aspects of their citizens' lives.

Over time, though, both the slackers and workaholics grew discontent. The slackers wanted more things, the workaholics more time. Both talked about work/life balance, but neither could achieve it. The pendulum of human behavior swings wildly.

By 2075, both groups had reverted to their previous state. They stayed that way, for a while.

LION AND LAMB

AT LAST, the bitter clash was over. Each side had fought hard until election day. Then the people spoke, and a winner emerged.

During the campaign, each side had vilified the other. Each had said a win by the other would doom everyone. Each side claimed only it could save the nation.

But now, as the dust settled, there was a moment of silence as it dawned on both sides that, despite their differences, they must still live together.

And so, wary but hopeful, they came together and began to talk.

ACKNOWLEDGMENTS

I want to thank my wife Liz, Libby Belle, Kathy Kennedy and Patti Normile for all their help and encouragement, Maggie Toerner for her wonderful cover design and Beth Anderson and Jon Virgi for their formatting.

I also want to extend grateful acknowledgment to the editors of *Friday Flash Fiction, Waves of Words, Bright Flash Literary Review, Culterate, FlashFlood* and *Down in the Dirt,* the literary magazines where the original versions of some of these stories appeared.

Don Tassone

ABOUT THE AUTHOR

After a long career in the corporate world, Don Tassone has returned to his creative writing roots. He is the author of two novels and nine short story collections. He and his wife Liz live in Loveland, Ohio. They have four children and 12 grandchildren.